Who Will Be My Valentine?

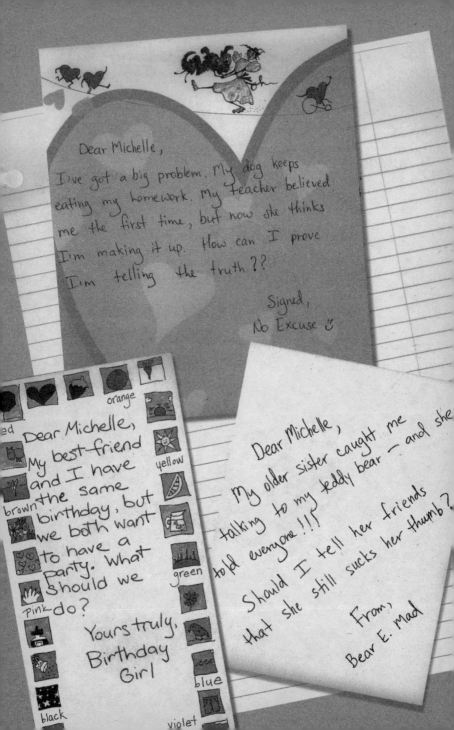

Dear Michelle,

I've got a big problem. My dog keeps eating my homework. My teacher believed me the first time, but now she thinks I'm making it up. How can I prove I'm telling the truth??

Signed,
No Excuse ☺

Dear Michelle,

My best-friend and I have the same birthday, but we both want to have a party. What should we do?

Yours truly,
Birthday Girl

orange
yellow
brown
green
pink
red
blue
black
violet

Dear Michelle,

My older sister caught me talking to my teddy bear — and she told everyone!!!

Should I tell her friends that she still sucks her thumb?

From,
Bear E. Mad

Who Will Be My Valentine?

by Jean Waricha

📖 HarperEntertainment
An Imprint of HarperCollins*Publishers*

A PARACHUTE PRESS BOOK

A PARACHUTE PRESS BOOK

Parachute Publishing, L.L.C.
156 Fifth Avenue
Suite 302
New York, NY 10010

Published by

HarperEntertainment

An Imprint of HarperCollins*Publishers*
10 East 53rd Street, New York, NY 10022-5299

ISBN 0-06-054085-0

First printing: January 2004

Printed in the United States of America

Visit HarperEntertainment on the World Wide Web at
www.harpercollins.com

10 9 8 7 6 5 4 3 2 1

Chapter One

"Come on, Michelle. Go for it!" my best friend, Cassie Wilkins, yelled from first base.

"You can do it!" my other best friend, Mandy Metz, called out from third.

It was Friday afternoon during gym class. We were in the middle of a major kickball game on the playground. The girls were playing against the boys.

Mandy brushed her curly dark hair out of her eyes and waited to run to home. If I made this kick, the girls would win the game!

Jeff Farrington was pitching. "Don't cry

too hard when you miss the ball!" he shouted, trying to make me nervous.

"Good luck, Michelle," Lionel Porter said—even though he was the catcher for Jeff's team. Lionel was always so nice.

"Thanks, Lionel." I shuffled my feet around, shaking them out. Stay calm, I told myself. Keep your eye on the ball.

Jeff rolled the ball to me—fast.

Whack! I kicked it as hard as I could with my sparkly purple sneakers.

The ball flew high over Jeff's head and bounced to the fence. My heart was pounding. Mandy and Cassie flew around the bases ahead of me.

Lionel shouted to Manuel Martinez, who was in the outfield, "Get the ball! Get the ball!"

But Manuel was too late. By the time he hurled the ball to second I was already jumping onto home plate.

"We did it!" Cassie slapped me a high five.

"We won!" Mandy yelled.

The three of us jumped up and down and hugged one another. Soon the other girls on our team were all cheering around us.

Mr. White, the gym teacher, blew his whistle. "Okay, kids, the period is almost over. Great game!" He motioned everyone inside.

I didn't really want to go back to our regular classroom. I liked the fresh February air. And gym was my favorite subject. I wished we could have gym all day long!

No such luck. Mrs. Ramirez, our third-grade teacher, was waiting for us in the hall. But I had to smile when I saw her. She was wearing her long dark hair in a French braid. And she had on a red scarf with tiny white hearts all over it.

"That's a pretty scarf," I told her. "Are you wearing it because Valentine's Day is coming soon?"

"That's right, Michelle," Mrs. Ramirez said with a smile. "Valentine's Day is such a fun holiday!"

Mrs. Ramirez thinks every holiday is fun. That's part of the reason I like her so much. Last Halloween she wore earrings shaped like pumpkins. And the day before winter break she wore a sweater that lit up like a Christmas tree!

I followed the teacher back to our classroom. My eyes almost popped out of my head when we got there. Mrs. Ramirez had decorated the whole room while we were playing in gym!

Huge red hearts were stapled to the bulletin boards at the back of the room. Red and white paper streamers were draped across the ceiling. Pink hearts hung on the windows. Little cupids surrounded the blackboard at the front of the room. It looked awesome!

"This is so cool!" Bailey Zimmerman said.

"I feel like I'm inside a Valentine's Day card!" Paige Alexander cried.

Everyone buzzed with excitement.

"Okay, class, settle down," Mrs. Ramirez said. "I have something to tell you."

I rushed to sit at my desk. It's the third seat in the third row.

"Can anybody guess why the room is decorated this way?" Mrs. Ramirez asked.

Louie Rizzoli raised his hand. "Is it because . . . Valentine's Day is next week?"

"Yes, it is!" Mrs. Ramirez said. "And we'll be working on a special Valentine's Day edition of the *Third-Grade Buzz*!"

The *Third-Grade Buzz* is our class newspaper. Everybody in the class helps write it. My job is to write the "Dear

Michelle" advice column. Kids send me letters with questions and I answer them. Each month I pick one letter to go into the *Buzz*. It's a lot of work and a lot of fun too!

"I have more news," Mrs. Ramirez said. "We're going to have a special Valentine's Day party next Friday."

The whole class cheered!

"Ooh! Ooh! Ooh!" Gracie Chin's hand shot up in the air.

"Yes, Gracie," Mrs. Ramirez said.

Gracie thought for a minute. "I forgot," she said.

Someone in the back of the room giggled. Gracie is always forgetting what she wants to say.

"Then let's continue," Mrs. Ramirez said. "We'll have cupcakes, punch, and a video at the party. You can sit with whomever you want. And we'll have art every afternoon, starting today, so you can make valentine cards for everyone in class and for your families."

I couldn't wait to start making cards— the sooner the better. Just giving some to my family alone meant I had to make a ton of them. That's because I live in a very full house.

There's my dad, Danny, and my two older sisters, D.J. and Stephanie. That makes three cards. My mom died when I was little, so Joey Gladstone moved in to help take care of us. He's my dad's best friend from college. That's four.

My uncle Jesse moved in too. And he got married to Aunt Becky. Then they had twin boys, Nicky and Alex. That's eight cards.

And I can't forget our golden retriever, Comet. I wouldn't want to leave him out— even if he can't read. That makes nine cards in all.

Julia "Bossy" Rossi raised her hand. "Mrs. Ramirez, do we have to make valentine cards for *everyone*?" she asked. "What if you don't want to make someone a card? Especially if you think that person is silly, stupid, and stuck-up." Julia glanced back from the seat in front of me and squinted her eyes.

I squinted back. Julia can be a real pain sometimes. She thinks she knows everything. And she's mad because *I* got picked to write the advice column for the *Buzz*—not her. But Mrs. Ramirez chose me fair and square!

"We have to make cards for everyone," Mrs. Ramirez told her, "especially since no one in this room is silly, stupid, or stuck-up."

Mrs. R. is a smart teacher, I thought. She started passing out red paper and showed us how to cut out the shape of a heart.

Cassie and Mandy leaned in close to me.

"You, Mandy, and I are sitting together at the party, right?" Cassie whispered.

"You bet," I said. Then I got an idea. "Hey, let's make a special valentine for Mrs. Ramirez," I whispered. "We can do it at my house one day after school."

"Sure," Mandy said. "I'll bring the paper."

Cassie giggled. "I'll bring the glue."

"I'll bring the glitter," I said with a big smile. I started cutting out a paper heart. First we won the kickball game, then I found out we're having art every day next week *and* a party. . . .

I can't wait for Monday to get here, I thought. Valentine's Week is going to rock!

Chapter Two

After school I checked my "Dear Michelle" letter box. It sits on the floor right outside our classroom. Part of my homework is to pick a letter and answer it for my column.

I stuck my hand inside the box and found three letters! I couldn't wait to read them.

When I got home I ran straight up to my room. I share it with Stephanie, but she wasn't home yet.

I sat at my desk and opened my backpack. I decided to do the easy homework first. I pulled out two math work sheets and finished them in ten minutes. Then I read four pages from my science book. Next I wrote ten sentences, using our new spelling words.

Finally I was ready to pick the letter for my column. I cleared my desk, took a deep breath, and read the first one:

Dear Michelle,
    How can I get my little brother to stop bothering me when my friends come over?
               Yours truly,
               Bugged-Out Big Sister

Hmm. This is a tough one. How should I answer it? I wondered. I thought and thought. Finally I began to write:

Dear Bugged-Out,
    How about letting your brother

play one game with you and then asking him to join you for a nail polish party. He'll probably find somewhere else to go pretty quickly. And that's my advice!

Love,
Michelle

I opened the next letter and read it:

Dear Michelle,

My mom makes me wear a suit every time we visit my grandma and grandpa's house. I want to go fishing with Grandpa, but my mom won't let me go in my good clothes. What should I do?

From,
Go Fish

This one is a snap! I thought.

Dear Go Fish,
  Why don't you take some old clothes with you? After you hang out with your grandma awhile, you can change your clothes and go fishing with your grandpa. And that's my advice!

  Love,
  Michelle

At last I opened the third letter:

Dear Michelle,
  I think a girl in my class is really nice. She's smart and good at sports. She has strawberry-blond hair and blue eyes. How can I get her to think I'm nice too? I'm too shy to talk to her.
  Sincerely,
  Shy Guy

13

This letter is perfect for the Valentine's Day part of the *Buzz!* I thought. I'm definitely going to use it. But first I have to answer it!

That was the tough part. This question was even harder than the one from Bugged-Out! I'd better put on my thinking cap.

"Michelle, time for dinner!" I heard Dad yelling from downstairs.

Maybe I'll think better on a full stomach, I thought. I ran downstairs to the dining room.

While Dad dished out the spaghetti, I sat in my seat and tucked a napkin into the neck of my T-shirt.

"How was school today, girls?" he asked.

"Fine," D.J. answered.

"Okay," Stephanie said.

Dad turned to me just as I slurped up a mouthful of spaghetti. I can't do the twist-on-your-fork way of eating spaghetti, so I use the vacuum way instead.

"What about you, Michelle?" he asked. "Was your day as exciting as your sisters'?"

I sucked the last strands of spaghetti into my mouth and nodded. I told everybody about my home run and about our valentine party on Friday. I stopped to vacuum up more spaghetti.

"How is your 'Dear Michelle' column going?" Aunt Becky asked.

"Get any juicy questions?" Stephanie said, wiggling her eyebrows.

"Well," I said slowly, "I *did* get this letter from a boy who thinks a girl in my class is nice. He wants her to think he's nice too. But he's shy and he's afraid to talk to her. It's a tough one. I could use a little help."

"Your uncle Jesse used to write me the sweetest poems on Valentine's Day," Aunt Becky said, "just to get me to like him."

She got all mushy and kissed Uncle Jesse on the cheek. Then she kissed Nicky and Alex on their noses.

"I guess it worked," Uncle Jesse said with a smile. "She liked me so much, she married me!"

"Poetry schmoetry," Joey said. "When I was in the third grade, I gave my girl-friend a present for Valentine's Day. I gave her my pet frog."

"A frog?" D.J. rolled her eyes. "I bet she wasn't your girlfriend for long."

"What's wrong with frogs?" I asked. "I think they're cute."

Dad cleared his throat. "Michelle, the answer to your question is simple," he said. "What do I always say is the best way to make friends?"

"Be yourself," Stephanie, D.J., and I answered together.

Everybody laughed. Then Stephanie

started talking about what happened at the mall today.

I got a lot of good advice, but whose advice should I give to Shy Guy: Aunt Becky's, Joey's, or Dad's?

Chapter Three

"Quiet please," Mrs. Ramirez said on Monday at school. She clapped her hands to get the class's attention. Everyone took a seat and the roar died down to a soft buzz.

Mrs. Ramirez cleared an area in the front of the room, then walked over to the windows. She was wearing a red sweater with a pink pin shaped like a heart on it.

"Okay, kids," she said. "Let's share how we're doing on our assignments for the *Buzz*. Who wants to go first?"

Jeff's hand shot up with the speed of

lightning. "I'll go!" He was already on his way to the front of the room before Mrs. R. had a chance to say it was okay. "I wrote a joke," he said. "Are you guys ready?"

"Go for it!" Lionel called out.

"What did the snowman say to his girlfriend on Valentine's Day?" Jeff paused for us to try and figure out the answer. Then he said, "'You're cool.' The snowman said, 'You're cool.' Get it?"

There were a lot of groans from the class. But Jeff thought it was funny. He wouldn't stop saying "you're cool" all the way back to his seat.

Mrs. R. smiled. "Thanks, Jeff. Who's next?"

Isabella Jackson and Lauren Kubo both raised their hands.

"We have to go together," Lauren said, "because we worked together. We wrote an essay about Valentine's Day."

They walked to the front of the room and stood side by side.

Lauren poked Isabella in the arm. "You have the paper."

"No, I don't," Isabella said. "You have it."

"Oh," Lauren said. "Um, never mind, Mrs. Ramirez. We're not ready yet."

"Thanks for volunteering, girls," Mrs. Ramirez said. "But please make sure you're ready tomorrow."

Next Mrs. Ramirez called on Sergei Petrovich.

Sergei was from Russia. He was still learning English. He walked to the front of the room and picked up a piece of chalk. He wrote the word *valentine* on the board.

"I made words from the letters in this word," Sergei explained. He wrote the words *tin* and *line* and *nine* on the board.

"Mrs. R.!" Julia shouted. "Sergei didn't finish. I can make more words using those letters. *Latin* and *vine* and *ten* and—"

"Very good," Mrs. Ramirez said. "Good idea, Sergei. Why don't we ask our readers how many words they can make with *valentine*?"

"What do you have for us, Michelle?" Mrs. Ramirez asked after Sergei sat down.

"I have a Valentine's Day question for my column," I said, walking to the front of the room. Good thing I figured out how to answer Shy Guy's letter over the weekend, I thought.

I read the letter aloud. Then I read my answer:

Dear Shy Guy,
My dad always tells me to try to be myself when I want to make new friends. Why not do that? And if you're nice to her, she'll know that you're a nice person. My aunt Becky

21

used to get sweet poems from my uncle Jesse. That made her like him so much, she married him! If none of this works, try giving the girl you like a frog. My uncle Joey said it worked for him! So it just might work for you. And that's my advice!

Love,
Michelle

I headed back to my seat, feeling pretty good about my answer . . . until I passed Julia's desk.

"That was the stupidest thing I've ever heard. I could could have given better advice," she whispered loud enough so everyone could hear.

"So who do you think Shy Guy is, Michelle?" Cassie asked me later in the lunchroom.

I took the last bite of my peanut-butter-and-banana sandwich. "I don't know. I was just trying to help. I didn't really think about it."

"A boy likes a girl in our class," Mandy said. "This is so exciting!"

Now that I thought about it, Mandy was right. This *was* exciting. "Let's think about who it might be right now," I said.

Mandy held out her hand. "Let me see Shy Guy's letter."

I pulled it out of my backpack and handed it to her.

Mandy took a sip of her chocolate milk and read the letter. "It says here that the girl Shy Guy likes has strawberry-blond hair and blue eyes." She looked up. "Who has strawberry-blond hair and blue eyes?"

"Michelle does," Cassie said, pointing her thumb at me.

"And so do some other girls," I added.

23

"Okay." Mandy looked at the letter again. "Mr. Shy Guy says she's good at sports. Who's good at sports in our class?"

Cassie shrugged. "Almost all the girls are."

"Yeah." I agreed. "Who won kickball last Friday?"

"We did!" Cassie gave me a high five.

Mandy checked the paper again. "Well, Shy Guy says that this girl is smart too," she said.

"So who do we know who is smart, good at sports, and has strawberry-blond hair and blue eyes?" Cassie asked.

Mandy gasped. "I know who it is!"

"Who?" I asked.

"It's you, Michelle!" Mandy cried.

Cassie started singing, "Michelle's got a *boy*friend . . . Michelle's got a *boy*friend."

"I do not!" I said. "It could be anybody in our class."

"No way," Mandy said. "You've got a secret admirer. I know about these things. My big sister had one once."

I gulped hard. I could feel my face getting hot.

I was really glad when the bell rang to go back to class.

Saved by the bell, I thought. That gave me a reason to stop talking. But I couldn't stop *thinking*. Could Cassie and Mandy be right about this? Did I really have a secret admirer?

Mrs. Ramirez led us back to our room and we started working on our Valentine's Day cards. I walked up to the supply table to get some glue.

When I returned to my desk, I found a folded piece of white paper on the floor under my seat. It was a note! Of course, the first thing I did was pick it up and read it.

Dear Michelle,
  Roses are red
  Violets are blue
  Monkeys are cute
  And so are YOU!
  Your Secret Admirer (Shy Guy)

I stared at the last five words. Wow! It was true what Mandy and Cassie had said at lunch.

I had a secret admirer.

But who was he?

Chapter Four

I looked around at the boys in my class. Who was my secret admirer? Who was Shy Guy? I wondered.

Could it be Spencer Erickson?

I hoped not.

Spencer had glued his hands together and was trying to get them unstuck.

Was it Moose Reilly?

Matthew "Moose" Reilly had two straws stuck in his nose and was making animal noises. How gross!

Mrs. R. was telling him to take them out of his nose—and next time to leave the straws downstairs in the cafeteria.

How about Louie "Chewy" Rizzoli?

He was trying to hide behind Sergei so that he could stuff a whole cupcake in his mouth before Mrs. R. could catch him eating in class. Pink drool was running down his chin. Yuck.

I didn't want any of these boys to be my secret admirer. And none of the boys in class seemed like he could write a mushy poem.

I needed Cassie and Mandy to help me figure this out.

They were both standing by the pencil sharpener at the back of the room.

I grabbed a pencil and headed straight for the sharpener. "Someone left this note under my desk," I whispered and handed it to Cassie.

"Whoa." Cassie quickly read the note, then gave it Mandy.

"Any idea who wrote it?" Mandy asked.

Before I could answer, Jeff called my name.

"What do you want?" I asked.

Jeff walked over to us. "Hold out your hand. I have a present for you."

"You do?" I asked and held out my hand.

Jeff reached into his pocket and took out a handful of red cinnamon heart-shaped candies and poured them into my hand.

"Thanks, Jeff," I said, surprised. "Those are my favorite!"

"It's cupid's poop!" Jeff doubled over with laughter and went back to his seat.

Mandy, Cassie, and I glared at him.

"Class, you're supposed to be working on your valentines," Mrs. Ramirez warned us. "Everyone, back to your seats."

Cassie plucked a candy out of my hand and popped it into her mouth. Mandy and I did the same. It tasted pretty good.

"Maybe Jeff is the one who likes you," Cassie whispered as we headed back to our desks.

I gave her one of my you've-got-to-be-kidding looks.

"You know, Michelle," Mandy added, "my big brother is always doing stupid stuff like that . . . to the girls he *likes*."

"Really?" I asked. "Do you think *Jeff* could have written that poem?" I stared at Jeff in disbelief.

"Maybe," Cassie said. "He's always teasing you. My mom says that's how you know when a boy thinks you're cute."

Could Jeff really have a crush on me? That would be pretty gross. But I tried to look on the bright side, like my dad was always telling me to do.

Jeff was funny. Sometimes his jokes made me laugh. And he was good at sports. Oh yeah, last week he sucked down a whole carton of milk in ten seconds and he didn't even throw up!

I guess he's not so bad, I thought.

Maybe I could give him a special card for Valentine's Day—since he was being so nice to me all of a sudden.

I took a piece of red construction paper, cut it into a heart shape, and wrote his name on it.

I'll make him a funny cartoon, I decided. He'll like that.

I turned the card over and drew two oranges dressed like cupids.

Then I made them say, "Orange you glad it's Valentine's Day?"

I flipped over the card again and traced the letters of Jeff's name with a stream of glue. Then I went to the supply table, got some gold glitter, and shook it onto the glue.

Julia turned around in her seat. "What are you doing?" she asked.

"None of your business," I told her.

Julia spotted the valentine on my desk. "That looks special. Who's it for?" she asked. "Who's it for?" she repeated when I didn't answer her.

I still didn't answer her.

"You'd better say it or else I'm going to tell Mrs. Ramirez that you're hogging all the glitter," Julia warned me.

I sighed. "Well, Julia, if you must know, it's for my secret admirer," I told her, "Jeff Farrington."

"Jeff is your secret admirer?" Julia asked. Her mouth hung wide open.

I nodded. "Maybe I'll even ask him to sit with me at the Valentine's Day party— if Cassie and Mandy don't mind."

Julia closed her big fat mouth. Then she squinted her eyes at me. "That's not fair! Why do *you* always get everything?" she said. "I'm making Jeff *my* secret admirer. He's going to sit with *me* on Valentine's Day!"

"You can't *make* someone be your secret admirer," I said.

"Oh, yeah?" Julia took out a large black marker and wrote "To Jeff" on the valentine on her desk. "Watch this!" she said, getting out of her seat.

I knew exactly where Julia was going— Jeff's desk. She was going to give Jeff his card now instead of on Friday. She was going to try to steal my secret admirer!

No way! I thought. I shook off the extra glitter on my card for Jeff. Then I turned around in my seat and slammed it on Jeff's desk behind me.

Julia slammed hers down at the same time.

Jeff stared at Julia and me.

I pushed my card forward. "Here, Jeff," I said sweetly. "Read my card first."

Julia reached over and shoved her card next to mine. "No, read mine first, Jeff," she said.

Jeff looked at my card, then at Julia's. Which one would he open first?

Chapter Five

Julia and I waited for Jeff to pick a card. Jeff reached across his desk and chose mine.

Yes! I thought. I won!

"Jeff Farrington!" Julia yelled. "Put that card down and open mine first!"

Jeff dropped my card like a hot potato and grabbed hers. "Uh, thanks, Julia," he said in a shaky voice.

"Julia!" Mrs. Ramirez said. "Back to your seat right now."

Julia looked very pleased with herself. She gave me one of her creepy looks as she passed me.

I tried to ignore her and watched Jeff open my card. A second later he was laughing.

"That's a good one, Michelle," he said. "'Orange you glad it's Valentine's Day?' Why didn't I think of that?"

Yes! I thought. Jeff likes my card better!

I gave Julia one of my biggest grins. I wasn't going to let her steal away my secret admirer—even if it *was* Jeff Farrington. He was *my* secret admirer and it was going to stay that way!

After school I met up with Mandy and Cassie outside the classroom.

"Did you see what happened?" I asked them. "Did you see how Julia tried to get Jeff to be her secret admirer?"

Mandy nodded. "Knowing Julia, she's not going to give up, either."

"She's just jealous, Michelle," Cassie

said. "You can't let her win. Jeff liked you first."

"I won't," I said, and we headed down the hall.

"I wish there was a way to make sure," Mandy said. "If Julia gets Jeff to be her secret admirer, she'll never let us forget it."

Cassie shrugged. "The only thing I can think of is what my mom says all the time. She says that the way to a man's heart is through his stomach."

Mandy giggled. "And your dad has a really big stomach. So he must love your mom a lot," she said.

The three of us left the building and walked to the playground. Jeff was already there on the swings. Manuel and Lionel were talking to him. Julia was sitting on the swing next to Jeff.

"There's Jeff," Mandy whispered. "I'll let you give him the double-chocolate-chip cookie from my lunch. I was saving it to eat on the bus ride home, but it's all yours if you want it."

I shook my head. "No, thanks," I told Mandy. I was going to do what my dad always tells me to do. "I'll just go over there and be myself. I'll be right back." I walked over to the swings.

"Thanks for the brownie, Julia," Jeff was saying. He licked the chocolate off his fingers. "Want to hang around with us after school?"

"Sure!" Julia said. The school bus arrived and the four of them started to leave. I'd have to follow Dad's advice later. Right now I needed something for Jeff's stomach!

"Wait!" I shouted. "I have something for you too, Jeff!" I ran back to where Mandy and Cassie were standing. I needed Mandy's cookie, quick!

But when I got there, Mandy was sticking the last bite into her mouth!

"Oh, no," I said. "You ate it."

"Sorry, Michelle," Mandy said. "I thought you didn't want it."

Uh-oh, I thought. Now what am I going to tell Jeff?

"So what did you want to give me?" Jeff asked me a few seconds later. Julia and Manuel stood behind him.

"Yeah, Michelle, what do you have to give him? I don't see anything. Were you just making it up?" Julia asked.

"No," I said. "It's just that I . . . um . . . I have something to give you *tomorrow*."

"That's right." Cassie nodded.

"She has something for you and it's really big," Mandy chimed in. "You'll see."

"Yeah, right." Julia tugged on Jeff's arm and pulled him away.

"Thanks, guys," I told my friends. "Now

all I have to do is come up with something big to give Jeff. Something bigger than that brownie Julia gave him."

"But what?" Cassie asked.

I didn't know. My head was empty.

Julia and her stupid brownie, I thought. But then it came to me.

I would make Jeff not just one little brownie but a whole tray of cookies!

Let's see Julia Rossi top that!

Chapter Six

The next day I made sure I got to school early. I was holding a plastic container of heart-shaped sugar cookies that Aunt Becky and Stephanie had helped me make the night before. We had tasted a few and they were really good. I couldn't wait to see Julia's face when I gave them to Jeff.

The only problem was, Jeff wasn't at school yet.

I found Mandy and Cassie on the swings on the playground.

"You brought cookies," Mandy said.

"Yup," I told her, "but they're for Jeff."

Cassie stuck her nose near the container. "They sure smell good," she said. "Do they look as good as they smell?"

Mandy nodded. "Can we see them, Michelle?"

I looked around for Jeff. He was nowhere to be found. Oh well, there was no harm in letting Mandy and Cassie see the cookies. I opened the container.

Cassie and Mandy peeked inside.

"Mmm. These look so yummy," Mandy said.

I glanced around once more to look for Jeff. No sign of him yet.

"Could I taste one, Michelle?" Mandy asked. "Just a little one?"

Cassie nodded. "Me too?" she begged. "I love the way you decorated them with pink frosting."

I stared at the container, then at my

friends. What difference could two cookies make? I still had a lot for Jeff.

"Well, okay," I said, "but just one."

Cassie and Mandy each grabbed a cookie and munched on it.

"Mmm. That was soooooo good!" Cassie cried. "Much better than what I ate for dinner last night—bean-curd-and-zucchini casserole. My mom said it was good for our digestion."

"Yuck," Mandy and I said together.

"I can still taste it," Cassie added. She smiled at me. "Michelle, do you think I could have *one more* cookie? Just to get the taste out of my mouth."

"Me too?" Mandy asked. "Just the thought of eating bean curd is making me sick to my stomach."

"Go ahead," I said. "By the way, what is bean curd?"

None of us knew.

Just then Bailey walked over to us. "Hey, Michelle, you brought cookies!" Bailey reached in and helped herself to one before I could stop her.

"Shhh!" I told Bailey. I didn't want the whole playground to find out that I had cookies.

But it was too late. Everyone around us heard "Michelle brought cookies!" Soon kids were dipping their hands into my container without even asking!

"No, wait," I said. But trying to stop a bunch of cookie-crazed kids was like trying to stop a herd of stampeding horses. After everyone had grabbed a cookie, I stood there with my plastic container and two cookies left.

The bell rang, and I took my two cookies and went to class. I put my container on Mrs. Ramirez's desk so I could take off my coat.

"Are you sharing your sugar cookies with me, Michelle?" Mrs. Ramirez asked. "That's so sweet!"

I gulped and nodded. I wanted to say no, but Mrs. Ramirez was so nice. Even if I had only one cookie left I probably would have given it to her.

I hung up my jacket and went to my desk. Just two minutes before the late bell and still no sign of Jeff. I glanced at the last cookie and my mouth watered. I almost hoped he wouldn't show up so I could eat it myself.

Just then I felt a tap on my shoulder. I turned around to see Jeff sitting at his desk.

"Hey, Michelle. What did you bring me?" he asked.

A cookie, I was about to say. But Julia "Bossy" Rossi grabbed it from the container and shoved it in her mouth.

"She *had* a few cookies," Julia said, chewing. "They were okay, but you should come over after school and try some more of my mom's brownies. She baked a whole tray of them."

"Awesome," Jeff said. "I'll be there."

"Tough luck, Michelle," Julia said with a grin.

Chapter Seven

After school that day Mandy, Cassie, and I sat in the den at my house to work on our special card for Mrs. Ramirez.

We had just finished cutting out pictures for a valentine collage from one of D.J.'s fashion magazines. We were going to paste them onto a huge piece of pink poster board that we had found in the basement.

"What should we write on Mrs. R.'s card?" Mandy asked. "How about something about her pretty clothes?"

I didn't say anything. Instead I was

petting Comet and thinking about Julia and Jeff. Jeff and Julia. Julia and Jeff. Even their names sounded like they went together.

"Hello! Earth to Michelle!" Cassie shouted at me. "You're a million miles away."

"I was figuring out what to do about Julia Rossi. Right now Jeff's probably over at her house, pigging out on brownies."

"Let's finish the card later," Cassie said. "This is serious. Julia is totally winning!"

Mandy laid the card on the floor. "We have to think of something that Jeff really likes. Something way cooler than brownies."

I stroked Comet's soft orange fur again. Sometimes petting him helped me get ideas.

"I've got it!" Cassie cried. "Didn't Jeff say last week that he really wanted . . . a dog?"

Mandy glanced at Comet, who was sitting by my feet.

"Don't even think about it," I said. "There's no way I am giving away Comet."

"Did I say anything?" Mandy asked.

I grabbed one of D.J.'s magazines and started flipping through it. "I need just one little idea. One thing that will make me the winner—not Julia."

"But what?" Cassie asked.

I stopped at a page in the magazine and gasped. The title of the article read "How to Look and Feel Like a Winner!"

"My dad always says that if you feel like a winner, then you *are* a winner!" I said and held up the magazine. "This might be just what I need to beat Julia!"

The three of us plopped down on the floor and began reading. The first thing I had to do was get a makeover. The article said it would make me a total winner!

49

Mandy looked at me. "I could cut your hair," she said. "Where are the scissors?"

I didn't think that was such a good idea. "We need a professional for that," I told my friends. "Or at least an older sister. Stay here for a minute."

I ran upstairs to D.J.'s room and knocked on the door. "D.J., I need your help!" I yelled.

D.J. opened the door with the phone in her hands. "Hold on a minute, Suzie," she said into the phone. "Is it homework?" she asked me.

"Nope. I need a makeover," I told her.

D.J. smiled. "Suzie, I'll call you back," she said into the phone. "We have a makeover emergency here."

I went to get Mandy and Cassie. The three of us sat on the bed next to D.J.'s makeup table. "Now, tell me, Michelle. What's this all about?" D.J. asked.

"It's about Jeff," Cassie explained. "He's Michelle's secret admirer and bossy Julia is trying to steal him."

"This sounds serious. But why do you think you need a makeover?" D.J. asked.

Mandy held out the magazine article.

D.J. took the magazine and studied the article. "Michelle, this article isn't about winning a competition. It's about feeling good about yourself."

I looked down at my shoes and kicked at my purple shoelaces. D.J. was right. Maybe a makeover was a dumb idea.

D.J. thought for a minute. "Well," she said, "if it will make you feel better, I'd be happy to help out."

"Cool!" I shouted. "Thanks, D.J."

D.J. took out her brush, blow-dryer, and hair spray. "Here are the tools you'll need," she explained. Then she showed me how to curl my hair in small sections using the brush and blow-dryer. She ran her hands through my hair and fluffed it out.

Wow, I looked really pretty.

Finally D.J. took her hair spray and gave my hair a good spray. It smelled like watermelon.

"Do mine," Cassie said.

"Mine too," Mandy added.

Soon we all had big, fluffy hair. Cassie tiptoed around the bedroom like a fashion model. This gave Mandy the giggles. Soon we were laughing so hard we almost ruined our new hairdos.

"Dad won't let you out of the house with makeup on," D.J. said, "but maybe we can find you something else to wear—something colorful. I'll bet some of Stephanie's old clothes will fit you."

We followed D.J. to my and Stephanie's room.

D.J. searched through Stephanie's closet.

"Aha!" she cried out after a few minutes. "Here's what I'm looking for." She held up a short orange velvet dress that Stephanie had worn when she was my age. The dress was pretty. But it was not something I would normally wear to school. It had long see-through sleeves and tiny orange flowers around the collar.

D.J. ducked back into the closet and came up with a pair of fancy black shoes to match.

"Awesome!" I said, slipping into the dress and the shoes. "It's a perfect fit!"

"But how do you *feel*?" Cassie asked me.

I turned and stared at myself in the full-length mirror on the door. I had brand-new hair and pretty clothes. . . .

"I feel like a winner!" I cried.

Chapter Eight

"Maybe I should wear my sneakers with this," I said the next morning in my room. "What do you think, Steph?"

Stephanie looked me up and down. "No way," she said. "That dress is so pretty. And your hair is so fancy. You'll ruin the look if you wear your purple sneakers."

"Okay, okay." I slipped into the black shoes D.J. had found for me. I turned to face Stephanie. "How is this?"

Stephanie gasped when she saw the whole outfit. "Awesome!"

"Thanks," I said. I stared at myself in

the full-length mirror that hung on the back of the door.

I had to admit it. With this velvet dress and these shoes I felt like a million bucks.

I should get dressed up more often, I thought. Not just for holidays and special assemblies at school.

"Julia Rossi, watch out!" I said into the mirror.

"What's that all about?" Stephanie asked, and I explained how Julia wanted to steal my secret admirer.

"You mean this is for a boy?" she said, shaking her head. "Well, in that case you can borrow my perfume." She took a small bottle off her dresser and slipped it into my backpack. "Angel Dew. It's a total boy-magnet," she said. "Don't tell Dad."

"Don't worry. I won't." I grabbed my stuff and headed downstairs to wait for the bus.

This was so cool. Not only was I feeling like a winner, I had a total boy-magnet in my backpack!

Julia Rossi didn't stand a chance!

Mrs. Ramirez smiled at me when I walked into the classroom later that morning. "I like the color of your dress, Michelle. It's very pretty."

"Thanks, Mrs. R.," I said. "I like what you're wearing too." She had on a fuzzy red sweater and a silky, red-and-white striped skirt.

I looked to see if Jeff had heard what Mrs. Ramirez had said about my dress, but he was busy making spitballs . . . with Julia!

Then I remembered Stephanie's perfume. I guess I had to use the boy-magnet.

I went to my desk and pulled out the bottle of Angel Dew. There were still a few minutes before class started, so I sprayed it on me.

Just then Lionel walked by my desk. I sure hoped that he didn't start to like me all of a sudden. He's not the reason I sprayed the boy-magnet perfume.

Luckily, he only sneezed. "Atchoo!"

"Hi, Lionel," I said.

Lionel seemed as if he had something to say, but he sneezed again before he could say it.

I took out my math homework and got ready for class to begin. Then I turned my head. I looked at Jeff from the corner of my eye.

"Hey, Michelle, got any cookies—atchoo!" He sneezed too—and all over my math homework. Yuck.

Then Jeff raised his hand. "Mrs. Ramirez, can I move my seat? Michelle stinks," he said.

Julia and a few other kids burst out laughing.

I knew my face was as red as a tomato. This wasn't how it was supposed to happen, I thought. As soon as I get home after school I'm going to tell Stephanie that her boy-magnet stuff doesn't work so hot in the third grade!

At least we have gym today, I thought. That should take my mind off this mess.

Class started and I pretended to be busy with my work. But mostly I stared at the clock.

Finally it was time for Mrs. Ramirez to bring us down to Mr. White. "Okay," she told the class. "You know the routine. Change into your sneakers if you're not already wearing them. Then line up by the door."

I saw Julia take off her shoes and slip on her sneakers.

I watched Cassie and Mandy do the same thing.

Then I stared down at my fancy black shoes in horror. Oh, no! I thought. I forgot my sneakers at home! I checked my backpack, but I knew they weren't in there.

"What's wrong?" Mandy asked me, and I told her.

"All I have are these stupid shoes!" I said.

Mr. White looked at my feet when the class entered the gym. "Sorry, Michelle. I guess you'll be sitting this one out. Try to remember your sneakers next time."

"Sorry, Mr. White." I sat on a bench and watched the teacher split the class into two teams. They were going to learn how to play volleyball today.

"Go, Julia!" I heard someone shout when the game began.

She scored a point for her team. Everyone was cheering her name, and Jeff slapped her a high five.

I touched my velvety dress and stared at my fancy shoes. Whose dumb idea was it to get a makeover anyway? I wondered.

Oh, right, I thought. It was mine.

Say the names of the pictures and sound out the letters to read Michelle's valentine card to you!

_____

_____

_____

Write Michelle's message here.

Answer to Michelle's message: Be My Valentine

Dear Michelle
c/o HarperEntertainment
10 East 53rd Street
New York, NY 10022

FIRST
CLASS
POSTAGE
REQUIRED

Chapter Nine

After gym and lunch we went back to Mrs. Ramirez's classroom to do math. I usually love math, but today I didn't want to do it. I wanted to think of something—anything—that would stop Julia from stealing my secret admirer. But what? I opened my notebook and started to doodle.

"Okay. Tell me what is six hundred and fifty divided by fifty . . . Jeff?" Mrs. Ramirez had started a math review.

"Uh . . . is it . . . ten?" Jeff guessed at the answer.

"Michelle?" Mrs. R. called on me.

I thought for a few seconds. "Thirteen," I answered.

"Correct. And Jeff, be sure to study your division before next week's test."

For the rest of the period I watched the clock. I couldn't wait to get home and change my clothes. The dress was starting to itch. Finally the bell rang and school was over.

"I have gymnastics class today. Got to go," Cassie said as she ran off and waved good-bye.

I packed up my backpack. Then Mandy and I walked out together.

"My brother is picking me up today," Mandy said. "He's taking me to buy new soccer shoes. Do you want to come with us? You could call your dad and ask if it's okay."

"No, thanks." I wasn't in the mood to go shopping.

Mandy started off, then turned back. "Remember, we need to finish the card for Mrs. R. I'll come over to your house at four-thirty, okay?"

"Okay," I said, but I was only half listening. "Can you call Cassie?"

Mandy nodded, then ran off.

I walked to the bus. I could see Jeff coming toward me, but after the stinky perfume, I didn't really want to talk to him. Besides I had no idea how to get him back as my secret admirer anyway. I walked faster.

"Wait, Michelle," he called after me. "Would you help me with my math homework today?"

I stopped. Could I believe my ears? Did Jeff really want me to help him with homework? This was perfect. I mean, why wouldn't he want to be my secret admirer if I helped him out a little?

"Sure, Jeff," I said. I noticed that Julia was watching us from the playground. This couldn't be better. "I just have to go home and change."

When the school bus dropped me off, I ran into the house and upstairs to change. I put on my favorite jeans, my favorite pink sweatshirt, and my sparkly purple sneakers. This was more like it. I felt so much better.

I passed by D.J.'s room and peeked inside.

D.J. and Stephanie were sitting on the bed, looking through magazines.

"How did it go, Michelle?" D.J. asked.

"I'm heading over to Jeff's house to study right now," I answered.

"Must have been the perfume," Stephanie said.

"Must have been the new outfit," D.J. added.

"Actually, it was the math," I said, running down the stairs.

"What do you think that means?" I heard Stephanie ask D.J.

I'd tell them all about it later.

"Hey, small fry, where are you headed in such a hurry?" Uncle Joey called from the living room. He held a rubber chicken in his hand, so I knew he was practicing his comedy act.

"I'm going to a friend's house to study, but I'll be home for dinner." I grabbed my books from the hall table and opened the front door.

"Okay, but don't be late. Your dad is making lasagna tonight!"

Jeff lives around the corner, so it took me just a couple of minutes to get there. I knocked on the door and smiled when Mrs. Farrington answered it.

"Well, hello there, Michelle," she said as

she opened the door. "Jeff told me you were coming over to help him with his math. That's so nice of you. I'll tell him you're here."

Mrs. Farrington stepped aside to let me in. She called out Jeff's name from the bottom of the stairs.

Jeff came running down. "Hey," he mumbled, looking at the floor.

He's acting awfully shy, I thought. He barely said hello.

"Come on." He led me downstairs to the family room.

I looked around for a desk or table. There was nothing but toys and games around. I spread out the math book and our homework papers on the floor.

"Let's start with multiples of fifty," I said. "That's what Mrs. R. went over today." I looked up and around for Jeff. He was sitting on the couch, bouncing a soccer ball on his knee.

I waited for Jeff to get with the program. Then I cleared my throat loudly.

Jeff looked up from his bouncing. "I don't get it," he grumbled.

"We haven't started," I told him. "Why don't you put the ball down and come over here?"

Jeff got up and stood next to me.

I tried again. "You see, you divide five hundred and fifty—" I looked up at Jeff, who was now holding a video game. I gave him one of my serious looks.

He stopped. "Math is too hard," he whined.

"You can do it," I said. "Just follow along." I pulled out his homework sheet and did the first problem for him.

Jeff watched me for a while, then went back to his game.

"Come on, Jeff!" I tried to explain how simple it was to divide.

"I don't get it," he whimpered. He walked back to the couch, sat down, and started bouncing the soccer ball again.

I looked at my watch. It was five o'clock already—just an hour until dinner. Every time I tried to get Jeff to think about math, he made up a reason not to.

I was getting pretty tired of this. I didn't want to miss out on my dad's lasagna. So I kept working and explaining.

Pretty soon I had finished the entire work sheet for him.

"Hey, thanks, Michelle," Jeff said. He jumped up and grabbed the sheet out of my hand. "Didn't you say something about having to leave for dinner soon?" He dropped the work sheet into his backpack and went back to his video game.

I couldn't believe it. Jeff just tricked me into doing his homework for him. What a creep!

I gritted my teeth. I wanted to tell Jeff exactly what I thought of him. But if I did, then Julia Rossi would win. And Jeff would sit with her on Valentine's Day. And I didn't want that, did I?

Chapter Ten

When I got to school on Thursday, I saw Cassie and Mandy whispering together on the school steps. I couldn't wait to tell them about how horribly Jeff had acted the night before.

They stopped talking when I joined them. Cassie stood with her arms folded over her chest and Mandy had her hands on her hips.

"Wait till I tell you about going over to Jeff's house," I said.

Cassie and Mandy glanced at each other. They didn't say a word. I knew something was wrong. I started to get that nervous feeling in my stomach.

"So now that you have a boyfriend, you forgot all about us," Mandy said with a serious look on her face.

"What are you talking about?" I asked, staring at both of them. I tried to think of a reason why they were acting like this.

"I guess you didn't remember we were supposed to meet at your house to finish Mrs. Ramirez's valentine," Cassie said. "We came to your house at four-thirty. Your uncle Joey said you went to a friend's house."

"Thanks a lot," Mandy added. "I rushed back from the mall for nothing! I didn't even get a chance to buy my new soccer shoes."

"I'm sorry, but . . ." I started to explain. Before I could finish, Cassie and Mandy turned away from me and headed into school.

They're really, really, *really* mad at me, I thought, walking into the building by myself. But I didn't *mean* to forget about our promise.

In class I tried to pass them a note. But every time I tried, they sent it back. Soon everyone around us knew we'd had a fight.

Julia leaned over my desk and said, "It looks like they're dropping you like poison ivy." She gave me one of her mean, smirky smiles.

School dragged on forever. Even seeing Mrs. Ramirez's pretty red boots didn't cheer me up.

When the bell finally rang, Mandy and Cassie walked out together.

I headed down the school steps and to the playground alone.

Jeff and Julia stood by the swings. Julia was handing Jeff another one of her mom's brownies. I watched Jeff grab it, then shove the whole thing in his mouth in one big bite.

When I walked by them, Jeff opened his mouth and stuck out his tongue. Chewed-up brown goop stuck to his teeth and ran down his chin. "Thanks for doing my homework, Michelle," he said through a mouthful of brownie.

Gross! I thought. I lost my two best friends for him?

The next day was Friday—the day of our valentine party. I woke up early . . . and kind of sad. What had started out as a great week had turned into something awful.

I put on jeans and my sweatshirt with the heart on it. I tried to smile at Dad when I came down for breakfast.

"Happy Valentine's Day," he said and kissed me on the forehead. He could tell something was bothering me. "Why so blue?" he asked, pouring me some orange juice.

I sighed. "My best friends are mad at me. And I decided I don't want my secret admirer to be my secret admirer anymore," I explained. "I'm going to tell him today."

"Don't worry," Dad said. "Best friends don't stay mad for long. And telling that boy the truth is a good idea," he added. "It's better if you let him know right away."

I got to school just when the late bell rang. Mandy and Cassie were whispering in the classroom. They didn't even say hi.

I guess they are still mad at me, I thought.

I did my schoolwork and tried not to feel too bad. Mrs. Ramirez had saved her prettiest outfit for today. She had on a red flowery dress and red shoes. She wore a red scarf around her hair.

Finally the lunch bell rang. I sat with Bailey and Paige in the lunchroom. They were nice, but it wasn't the same as sitting with Cassie and Mandy. Soon lunch was over and it was time for the party.

When I got back to class, I saw that Mrs. R. had moved all the desks to the side. Comfy-looking blankets were piled in the center of the room. She was pouring punch into small red cups lined up on her desk. A large plate of pink cupcakes sat next to the punch.

Mrs. Ramirez settled us down on the blankets. "After we've had our cupcakes and punch, you all can give out your valentines. Everyone get comfortable."

I moved behind Jeff. I took a deep breath and tapped him on the shoulder. Out of the corner of my eye I could see Julia sneaking toward us. "Jeff, I'm very sorry, but I don't want you to be my secret admirer anymore." There, I had said it. Boy, did I feel better. It was as if a huge stone had been lifted off the top of my head.

Jeff's eyes widened. "What are you talking about, Michelle? I think you've been eating too many candy hearts." That made him laugh.

"You mean you're not my secret admirer?" I asked.

"No way!" Jeff cried.

"I knew it!" Julia said. She had been listening to us the whole time. "Now you can be my secret admirer. And we'll sit together at the party."

"Double no way," Jeff said. "You girls are crazy. I'm sitting with Manuel and Lionel."

Jeff couldn't get away from us fast enough.

Julia stuck her nose in the air and sat down next to Gracie. She acted as if she had planned to sit with her all along.

Cassie and Mandy were sitting on a beige blanket close by, but I sat all by myself.

I had thought Valentine's Week was going to be totally awesome. But instead, it had turned out to be one big disaster!

Chapter Eleven

Mrs. Ramirez handed out the cupcakes, then served the punch.

One at a time we got up and passed out our valentine cards. While I waited my turn, I wondered how I ever could have believed that Jeff was my secret admirer.

But if Jeff wasn't my secret admirer, then who was? I looked around the room. *Someone* had left that poem under my desk.

It was almost my turn to give out valentines. Lionel was still handing out his, but he was just about finished. He walked up to me holding his last card. In

his other hand he held something else—
something greenish and small.

"Happy Valentine's Day, Michelle,"
Lionel whispered. His face turned pink.
He was blushing.

"Thanks, Lionel. What's in your hand?"
I asked.

Lionel held out his hand and showed
me. "It's a ceramic frog. I made it for you.
My mom helped me paint it." He sat down
next to me. "Remember the advice you
gave in your 'Dear Michelle' column? Well,
here's your frog."

"Lionel, are you my secret admirer?" I
asked quietly. "Did you write me that poem?"

Lionel nodded and smiled at me.

I was glad Lionel was my secret admirer.
He was the nicest boy in the whole third
grade.

"Thanks for the poem," I said. "Do you
want to sit together at the party?"

Lionel got up. "I'd like to, but I already promised Jeff and Manuel I'd sit with them."

"That's okay, Lionel," I said. "I'll see you later. And thanks for the frog. It's really cool."

Lionel grinned and went over to the blue blanket where Jeff and Manuel had set up their things. Jeff was tearing open his valentines and making them into paper airplanes.

Lionel made me feel a little better. But I still didn't have anyone to sit with at the party. I put the ceramic frog on my desk.

Julia watched me. "That's cute. Where'd you get it? Who gave it to you?" she asked.

"Lionel made it for me." I showed it to her. "It's a frog."

"Oh!" was all that Julia said. Then she turned around and began to open her Valentine's Day cards.

Mrs. Ramirez called my name and told

me it was my turn to pass out valentines.

I walked around the room, giving everyone their card. I had made one for everyone in the class, even Julia. When I'd finished, I heard someone call my name.

"Michelle! Michelle!" I turned around to see Cassie and Mandy coming toward me.

"How come you're not sitting with us?" Mandy asked. "Are you mad at us? You didn't even say hi this morning."

"No way," I said, shaking my head. "I'm not mad. I thought that you were still mad at me. Does that mean we're friends again?"

"We're friends forever," Cassie said.

"And best friends can't stay mad at each other," Mandy added.

The three of us hugged one another.

Then Mandy reached into her pocket and pulled out a Valentine's Day card. It said "To Mrs. Ramirez" on the front.

"Here." Mandy handed it to me. "We

want you to sign it. Cassie and I made it last night. It's going to be from the three of us."

"Wait right here," I told them. I ran to the coat closet and came back with the big pink valentine that we had started together. "I finished it last night," I explained. I held up the card so they could read it.

It said:

Roses are red.
Violets are blue.
Mrs. R. is the best.
We LOVE you!

It was decorated with roses and hearts covered with gold glitter. I had cut out pictures of all the pretty clothes Mrs. R. had worn for Valentine's Week. There were red shoes, a red dress, a red sweater, a striped skirt, and a pretty red scarf with hearts on it. Then I glued sequins all around the border. At the bottom I drew a long dark line for our names.

"Wow!" said Cassie. "That looks great!"

I held out my pen and Cassie and Mandy signed their names.

"If we are all finished handing out valentines," Mrs. Ramirez called out, "we can watch a video."

"Mo-*vie*, mo-*vie*, mo-*vie*!" the class cheered.

"We have two more valentines to give out, Mrs. R.," I said.

Cassie, Mandy, and I linked arms and brought our valentines up to the front of the room.

"What beautiful cards," Mrs. Ramirez said. "Thank you, girls."

I looked at Julia, who was frowning. But she didn't seem mad. She seemed as if she wished she'd made Mrs. Ramirez a special card too.

Should I? I wondered. Oh, why not? I thought. It's Valentine's Day!

"Um, the cards are from Julia too," I added quickly. "She forgot to sign them."

Julia gave a big grin and ran up to the front of the room to sign her name. "Thanks, Michelle," she whispered.

"You're welcome," I whispered back.

"Happy Valentine's Day, class!" Mrs. Ramirez announced.

I sneaked a peek at Lionel, who was smiling at me. Cassie and Mandy were laughing and drinking punch. Even Julia was in a good mood!

Yup, I thought. Valentine's Day turned out to be pretty happy after all!

Hi, I'm Michelle Tanner!

I write the advice column for my school newspaper, the Third-Grade Buzz. A letter can tell you a lot about a person. But the person who wrote me the letter on the next page forgot to sign it. Can you help me figure out which kid in Mrs. Ramirez's class wrote this letter?

February 14, 2003

Dear Michelle,

This is my first Valentine's Day in America. I come from Russia. The party at school was very fun. But I did not get many cards. Will you send me one?

Happy Valentine's Day!

From,

Now that we know Sergei wrote the letter, let's make him Valentine's Day cards!

Here's what you need:

A sheet of newspaper, red construction paper, a pencil, glue, glitter, a black marker

Here's what you do:

Step 1: Open your newspaper sheet and place it on a flat surface. This will be your working area.

Step 2: Take the construction paper and hold it in front of you the long way. Fold it in half to make your card.

Step 3: Take your pencil and draw a heart on the front of your card. Now open your glue bottle and squirt the glue along the outline of the heart you just drew.

Step 4: Then sprinkle some glitter on the glue heart. Make sure you do this over the newspaper. It can get messy!

Step 5: Let your glue dry for thirty minutes. Then open your card. Use your marker to write a message to Sergei inside!

Step 6: Put this address on the envelope:

(Don't forget to put your own name and address here!)

stamp
goes
here

Sergei Petrovich
c/o Dear Michelle
HarperEntertainment
10 East 53rd Street
New York, NY 10022

Do you need some advice—or want to ask me a question? I may be able to answer you in one of my future columns! I wish I could answer all of your letters, but I get too many! I would still love to hear from you. Write to me, Michelle, at:

Dear Michelle
c/o HarperEntertainment
10 East 53rd Street
New York, NY 10022

You can use the cool postcard in this book. It already has the address on it!

Here's a sneak peek at

#4 I've Got Bunny Business!

Max and I sat on the steps of the bunny building. I buried my head in my hands. The sun shone in the bright blue sky. It was a perfect spring day. But Max and I felt horrible! Where was our bunny, Pixie?

"The games are going to start without us!" Max cried. "And we still don't know where Pixie is!"

"We won't find Pixie by sitting around and feeling sorry for ourselves!" I stood up and held out my hand.

"Okay, partner," he said, grabbing it. "Let's find that bunny!" Max wandered off to look through a patch of red and yellow tulips blooming nearby. "Wow!" he shouted.

"Pixie!" I raced over. "Did you find her?"

"No," Max said. "But look." He picked up a small green frog sitting next to a red tulip. "But he's so cool!"

"You're right," I said, staring at the frog. "But we still have to find Pixie."

Think, brain, think! I told myself. Where is the only place we haven't looked?

"I've got it!" I yelled. "The closet in the bunny room! We forgot to look in there!"

"Let's check it out," Max said. He put the frog in his jacket pocket and followed me back to the bunny room.

When we got there, I rushed into the big storage closet. Large metal shelves on the walls held supplies for the animals. Big bags of bunny chow and hay sat on the floor. One of the bags was open.

And there munching on a strand of hay . . . was Pixie!

Pixie looked up at us and wiggled her nose.

"I found her!" I called to Max. I had never been so glad to see a bunny in my entire life!

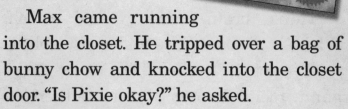

Max came running into the closet. He tripped over a bag of bunny chow and knocked into the closet door. "Is Pixie okay?" he asked.

The door began to swing closed.

"Max, watch out!" I cried. Too late! The door shut with a slam.

Max grabbed the doorknob and tried to turn it. But it wouldn't budge!

"Oh, no, Michelle," Max said. "We're locked in!"